# The 20-Minute Intermediate Piano Workout

By Douglas Riva

# Introduction

SO MANY PIANISTS have been helped to play with greater accuracy, control and ease—in easy, step-by-step lessons lasting just 20 minutes at a time—by *The 20 Minute Piano Workout*, that the author, Douglas Riva, has now written a supplementary text by popular demand. Welcome to the *The 20 Minute* **Intermediate** *Piano Workout*.

If you've already gone through the earlier volume, you're ready to develop your technique even further, moving from an intermediate level to more advanced kinds of piano playing. If this is your first encounter with the *20 Minute* series, here are a few words about the method.

This method is organized into 18 Weeks (or Chapters). Each Week is devoted to different aspects or problems of piano playing—patterns, chords, double notes, repeated notes, octaves, and more. After completing each Week, you will receive a performable piece that contains some of the technical difficulties encountered in the Drills.

Each Week is accompanied by a Practice Calendar to organize your practice time. It will show you when and how to practice the Drills in that Week. Try to make the most of each 20 minute period, but do not expect too much of yourself in just one or two sessions. As you practice, you will slowly but surely find—through full attention and adherence to the regimen—that your fingers will respond more quickly and fluidly to the musical challenges on the page.

If this book is too difficult for you, use the first volume to increase your playing level before turning to this volume. When you have completed both volumes, you will be more prepared to tackle new and difficult music than you ever thought possible! GOOD LUCK!

DOUGLAS RIVA *received his musical education at the Juilliard School in New York and at the Academia Marshall in Barcelona. His most important teachers were Eugene List and Mercè Roldós. In 1982, he was invited by the Town Hall Foundation to make his New York debut at Town Hall, performing Granados' Goyescas. Two years later, he presented the World Premiere of unknown and unpublished works by Granados in Barcelona, at the request of the composer's daughter.*

*Dr. Riva has recorded for Radio WQXR–New York, WXTV– New York, and the Voice of America in the United States—and for Radio Nacional de España, Catalunya Radio, TV-3, Radio Miramar, and Radio Ser in Spain. He is an Associate Professor at Pace University and the Hoff-Barthelson Music School, and he has lectured at Harvard University, New York University, the New School, and Wells College. He is a Contributing Editor of Keyboard Classics, and his recordings have been released by the Musical Heritage Society; the Keystone Music Roll Company; and Centaur Records, which recently released his recording of The Unknown Granados.*

# WEEK

# 1

| Monday | Drill A, First Reading, 5 Minutes<br>Drill A, Second Reading, 5 Minutes<br>Drill B, First Reading, 5 Minutes<br>Drill C, First Reading, 5 Minutes |
|---|---|
| Tuesday | Drill A, Second Reading, 5 Minutes<br>Drill B, First Reading, 5 Minutes<br>Drill B, Second Reading, 5 Minutes<br>Drill C, First Reading, 5 Minutes |
| Wednesday | Drill A, Third Reading, 5 Minutes<br>Drill A, Fourth Reading, 5 Minutes<br>Drill B, Third Reading, 5 Minutes<br>Drill C, Second Reading, 5 Minutes |
| Thursday | Drill A, Fourth Reading, 5 Minutes<br>Drill B, Fourth Reading, 5 Minutes<br>Drill B, Fifth Reading, 5 Minutes<br>Drill C, Third Reading, 5 Minutes |
| Friday | Drill A, Fifth Reading, 5 Minutes<br>Drill B, Sixth Reading, 5 Minutes<br>Drill C, Third Reading, 5 Minutes<br>Drill C, Fourth Reading, 5 Minutes |
| Sat/Sun | Drill A, Fifth Reading, 5 Minutes<br>Drill B, Seventh Reading, 5 Minutes<br>Drill C, Fourth Reading, 10 Minutes |

# "Step by Step"

**First Reading**

Right hand alone, measures 1–8. Left hand alone, measures 9 and 10. Then go back to the right hand alone, measures 11–16. Play legato.  ♪ = 100–126.

**Second Reading**

Follow the directions for the First Reading, but increase the tempo to ♪ = 138–176.

**Third Reading**

Left hand alone, measures 1–8. Right hand alone, measures 9 and 10. Then go back to the left hand alone, measures 11–16.  ♩ = 63–88.

**Fourth Reading**

Hands together.  ♩ = 63–88.

**Fifth Reading**

Hands together. Increase the tempo to  ♩ = 96–112.

# Drill A

# "Thumbs Up"

THIS DRILL will help you make your thumbs as flexible as possible. Concentrate on making the thumbs move with ease and freedom.

**First Reading**
Right hand alone. Play *p*.  ♩ = 72–88.

**Second Reading**
Left hand alone. Play *p*.  ♩ = 72–88.

**Third Reading**
Hands together. Play *p*.  ♩ = 72–88.

**Fourth Reading**
Hands together. Play all notes staccato and *mf*.  ♩ = 72–88.

**Fifth Reading**
Hands together. Move the right hand up one octave. Move the left hand down one octave. Play slurs as written. Play *f*.  ♩ = 88–96.

**Sixth Reading**
Hands together. Move the right hand up two octaves. Play the left hand as written. Play staccato and *mp*.  ♩ = 88–108.

**Seventh Reading**
Hands together. Play both hands as written. Play slurs as written. Play *mp*.  ♩ = 108–120.

# Drill B

# "Funny Fingers"

ANYONE who hears you practice this Drill is sure to laugh! They will find it very difficult to believe that you could be improving your technique while you are playing so many "wrong" notes. Let them laugh. Meanwhile, you will be increasing your agility. The trick here is to play the bottom notes of the ascending scales legato and the top notes of the descending scales legato—and to play as lightly as possible. Three major scales are shown in the Drill, but you could try the same technique on any major or minor scale.

**First Reading**

Hands together. Play as written. Play *p*. ♪ = 120–126.

**Second Reading**

Hands together. Increase the tempo to ♩ = 144–160 ( ♩ = 72–80).

**Third Reading**

Hands together. Increase the tempo to ♩ = 96–108.

**Fourth Reading**

Try the same technique on any three different scales. ♩ = 96–108.

# Drill C

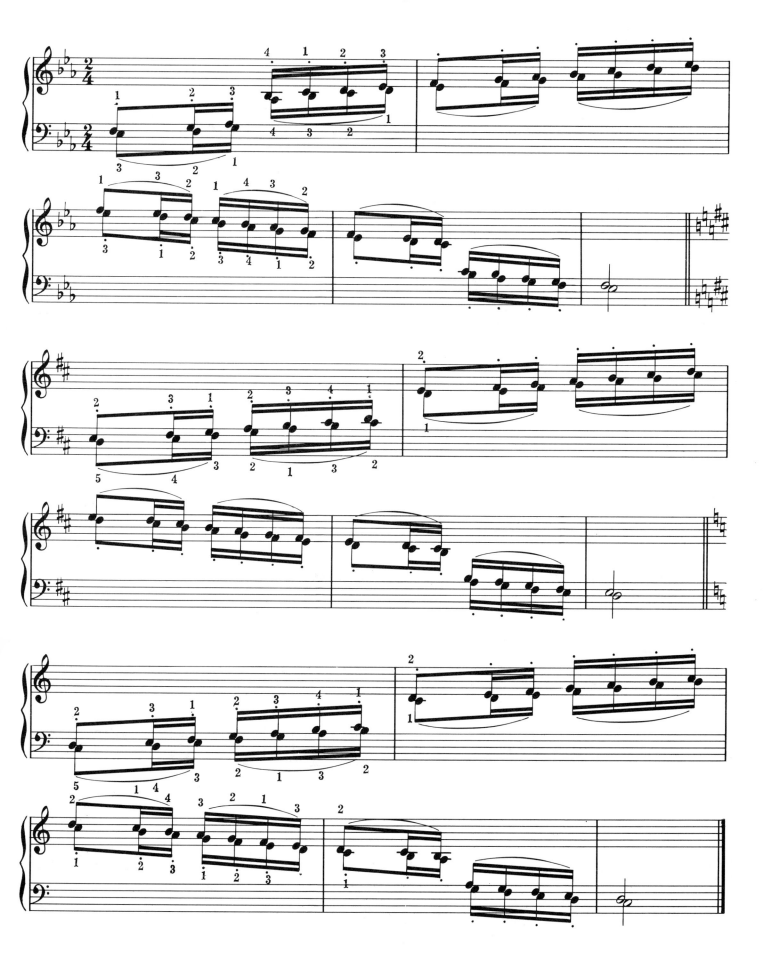

# Sonata

Julián Prieto

Spiritoso ( ♩ = 88-92)

13

# Week
# 2

| | |
|---|---|
| **Monday** | Drill A, First Reading, 5 Minutes<br>Drill A, Second Reading, 5 Minutes<br>Drill B, First Reading, 5 Minutes<br>Drill C, First Reading, 5 Minutes |
| **Tuesday** | Drill A, Third Reading, 5 Minutes<br>Drill B, First Reading, 5 Minutes<br>Drill C, Second Reading, 5 Minutes<br>Drill C, Third Reading, 5 Minutes |
| **Wednesday** | Drill A, Fourth Reading, 5 Minutes<br>Drill B, Second Reading, 5 Minutes<br>Drill C, Fourth Reading, 10 Minutes |
| **Thursday** | Drill A, Fifth Reading, 5 Minutes<br>Drill B, Third Reading, 5 Minutes<br>Drill C, Fourth Reading, 5 Minutes<br>Drill C, Fifth Reading, 5 Minutes |
| **Friday** | Drill A, Sixth Reading, 5 Minutes<br>Drill B, Fourth Reading, 5 Minutes<br>Drill C, Sixth Reading, 10 Minutes |
| **Sat/Sun** | Drill A, Seventh Reading, 5 Minutes<br>Drill B, Fourth Reading, 10 Minutes<br>Drill C, Seventh Reading, 5 Minutes |

THIS DRILL will help you become familiar with varying distances between notes played by the same fingers. While it appears to be easy to play, it is more difficult than you might think.

**First Reading**
Right hand alone. Use only the second and third fingers. Play *mf*. ♩=88–120.
**Second Reading**
Left hand alone. Use only the second and third fingers. Play *mf*. ♩=88–120.

**Third Reading**
Hands together. Use only the second and third fingers. Play *mf*. ♩=88–120.

**Fourth Reading**
Hands together. Use only the third and fourth fingers. Play all notes staccato and *p*. ♩=88–120.

**Fifth Reading**
Hands together. Use only the fourth and fifth fingers. Play slurs as written. Play *p*. ♩=88–120.

**Sixth Reading**
Hands together. Use only the third and fourth fingers. Move the right hand up one octave. Move the left hand down one octave. Play slurs as written. Play *mp*. ♩=88–120.

**Seventh Reading**
Hands together. Use only the fourth and fifth fingers. Play as written. Play staccato and *mf*. ♩=88–120.

# DRILL A

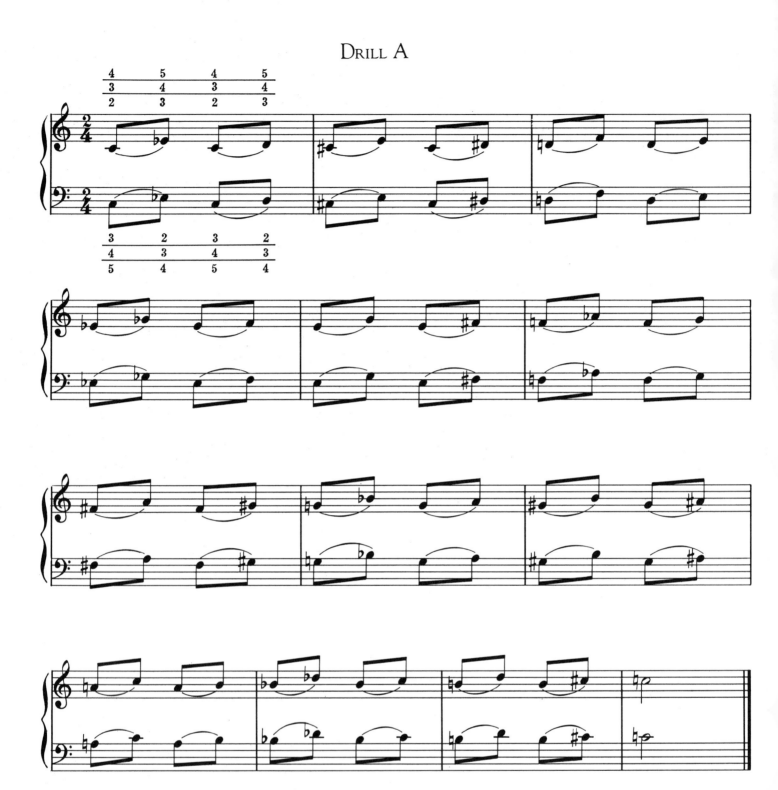

# "Automatic Fire"

ALTHOUGH it may appear somewhat confusing at first glance, this Drill is nothing more than several scales divided between the hands. The right hand plays the notes with the stems pointing upward, and the left hand plays the notes with the stems pointing downward. Try to make the Drill sound as if you were playing it with only one hand. Although the dynamic marking is *p,* you might also try *pp.*

**First Reading**
Play legato. ♪ = 116–132.

**Second Reading**
Play legato. ♪ = 138–152.

**Third Reading**
Play staccato. ♪ = 160–184 ( ♩ = 80–92).

**Fourth Reading**
Play legato. Increase the tempo to ♩ = 96–116.

# Drill B

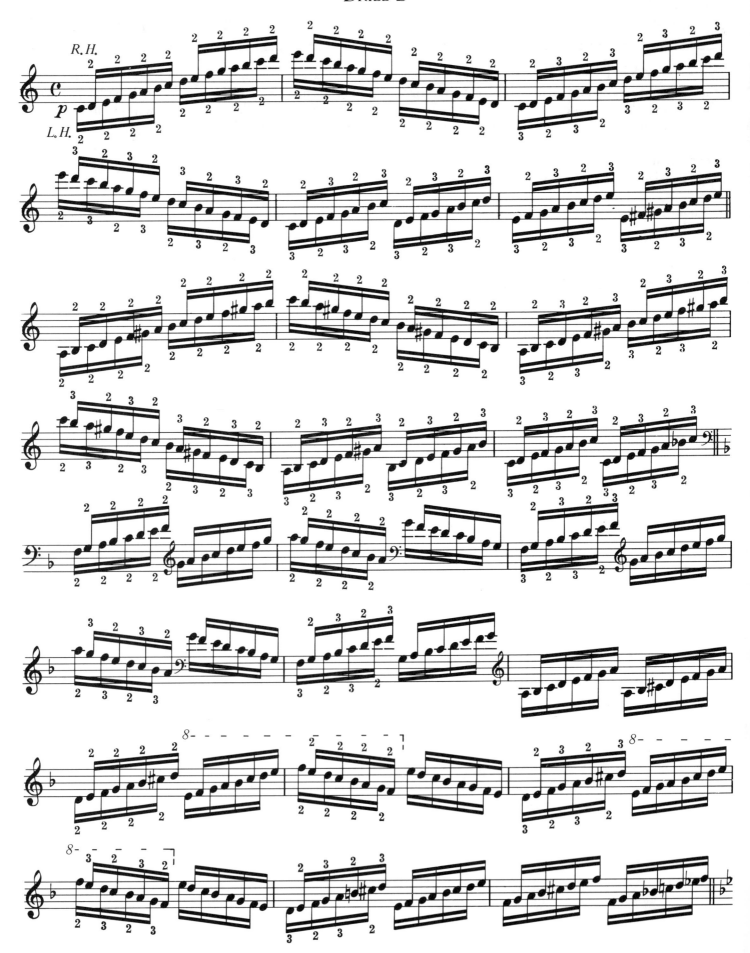

23

ALTHOUGH this Drill is a technical study, remember that it is also a piece of music. Try to make it sound like a ballet scene—light and flowing.

**First Reading**
Right hand alone. Follow the dynamic markings. Play legato. ♪ = 112–132.

**Second Reading**
Right hand alone. Follow the dynamic markings. Play legato. ♪ = 144–184.

**Third Reading**
Left hand alone. ♪ = 144–184.

**Fourth Reading**
Hands together. ♪= 112–132.

**Fifth Reading**
Hands together. Increase the tempo to ♪ = 144–184.

**Sixth Reading**
Hands together. Instead of emphasizing the pulse of each eighth note, group three eighth notes together into one dotted quarter note ( ♫♪ = ♩. ), resulting in two pulses per measure. ♩.= 60–76.

**Seventh Reading**
Hands together. Increase the tempo to ♩.= 80–88.

# Drill C

**Moderato**

*(continued on next page)*

# Bagatelle

## *Opus 33, No. 2*

Ludwig van Beethoven

**Scherzo**
**Allegro** ( ♩. = 66)

Minore

28

# WEEK
## 3

| | |
|---|---|
| **Monday** | Drill A, First Reading, 5 Minutes<br>Drill A, Second Reading, 5 Minutes<br>Drill B, First Reading, 5 Minutes<br>Drill B, Second Reading, 5 Minutes |
| **Tuesday** | Drill C, First Reading, 10 Minutes<br>Drill A, Third Reading, 5 Minutes<br>Drill A, Fourth Reading, 5 Minutes |
| **Wednesday** | Drill B, Third Reading, 5 Minutes<br>Drill B, Fourth Reading, 5 Minutes<br>Drill C, Second Reading, 5 Minutes<br>Drill A, Fifth Reading, 5 Minutes |
| **Thursday** | Drill A, Fifth Reading, 5 Minutes<br>Drill A, Sixth Reading, 5 Minutes<br>Drill B, Fifth Reading, 5 Minutes<br>Drill C, Third Reading, 5 Minutes |
| **Friday** | Drill A, Seventh Reading, 5 Minutes<br>Drill B, Fifth Reading, 5 Minutes<br>Drill B, Sixth Reading, 5 Minutes<br>Drill C, Fourth Reading, 5 Minutes |
| **Sat/Sun** | Drill A, Seventh Reading, 5 Minutes<br>Drill B, Sixth Reading, 10 Minutes<br>Drill C, Fourth Reading, 5 Minutes |

# "In Black and White"

### First Reading

Right hand alone. Play measures 1–4 and 7–8 only. Use the fingering marked in the music. Play legato and *p*.
𝅘 = 126–144 ( ♩ = 63–72).

### Second Reading

Left hand alone. Play measures 5–6 only. Use the fingering marked in the music. Play legato and *p*.
𝅘 = 126–144 ( ♩ = 63–72).

### Third Reading

Right hand alone. Play measures 1–4 and 7–8 only. Practice each beat with the following rhythmic variation. Play legato and *p*.

Hold each note with a fermata (𝄐) and play the other three notes of the beat quickly.

### Fourth Reading

Left hand alone. Measures 5–6 only. Practice each beat with the same rhythmic variation you used in the Third Reading. Play legato and *p*.

### Fifth Reading

Right hand alone. Play the complete Drill as written. ♩ = 76–92.

### Sixth Reading

Left hand alone. Play the complete Drill as written ♩ = 76–92.

### Seventh Reading

Hands together. Play as written. ♩ = 76–92.

# Drill A

# "Skip to My Waltz"

THE TEMPO indication, *Mouvement de valse*, may not give you a very clear idea of the exact tempo for this Drill, however it does give us a very clear idea of the mood. A *valse* (waltz) is a graceful and elegant dance, with a strong accent on the first beat of each measure. Throughout the Drill, the left hand plays an accompaniment to the melody in the right hand. Typical of many waltz accompaniments, this Drill has many skips between the first and second beats of each measure. In order to land on the proper note for the second beat, you will have to watch your left hand when you first begin to practice. However, try to play it "by feel" as soon as possible.

**First Reading**
Left hand alone. ♩ = 112–132.

**Second Reading**
Right hand alone. ♩ = 112–132.

**Third Reading**
Left hand alone. Increase the tempo to ♩ = 144–168.

**Fourth Reading**
Hands together. ♩ = 112–132.

**Fifth Reading**
Hands together. ♩ = 144–168.

**Sixth Reading**
Hands together. ♩. = 72–80.

# Drill B

# "An International Slur"

$T$HIS DRILL was created by a respected pianist and composer of the nineteenth century, Carl Reineke. There is a certain similarity between this Drill and an etude by Adolf Henselt, *"Si oiseau j'étais"* ("If I Were a Bird"). Both pieces have the same time signature and a similar mood. This Drill is much easier than Henselt's long and difficult study, but both have a characteristic "flutter" appropriate to the title of Henselt's etude. Notice that a two-note slur occurs on almost every beat in Drill C. The second note of each pair should be played both shorter and softer than the first.

**First Reading**
> Hands together. ♩ = 104–132.

**Second Reading**
> Hands together. ♩ = 144–176.

**Third Reading**
> Hands together. ♩ = 180–196.

**Fourth Reading**
> Hands together. ♩. = 72–80.

# Drill C

# Allegro in F Minor

C.P.E. Bach

# WEEK 4

| | |
|---|---|
| **Monday** | Drill A, First Reading, 5 Minutes<br>Drill A, Second Reading, 5 Minutes<br>Drill B, First Reading, 5 Minutes<br>Drill C, First Reading, 5 Minutes |
| **Tuesday** | Drill A, Second Reading, 5 Minutes<br>Drill A, Third Reading, 5 Minutes<br>Drill B, First Reading, 5 Minutes<br>Drill C, Second Reading, 5 Minutes |
| **Wednesday** | Drill A, Fourth Reading, 5 Minutes<br>Drill B, Second Reading, 5 Minutes<br>Drill C, Third Reading, 5 Minutes<br>Drill C, Fourth Reading, 5 Minutes |
| **Thursday** | Drill A, Fifth Reading, 5 Minutes<br>Drill B, Third Reading, 5 Minutes<br>Drill C, Fourth Reading, 5 Minutes<br>Drill C, Fifth Reading, 5 Minutes |
| **Friday** | Drill A, Sixth Reading, 5 Minutes<br>Drill B, Fourth Reading, 5 Minutes<br>Drill C, Fifth Reading, 10 Minutes |
| **Sat/Sun** | Drill A, Seventh Reading, 10 Minutes<br>Drill B, Fourth Reading, 5 Minutes<br>Drill C, Fifth Reading, 5 Minutes |

# "Wind Chimes"

THIS DRILL is marked *leggiermente*, meaning light or airy; and this is the perfect description of how it should sound. Even when playing *f,* you can still get a light tone.

**First Reading**

Right hand alone. Play *leggiero*—that is, in between legato and staccato. ♪ = 120–132

**Second Reading**

Right hand alone. Increase the tempo to ♪ = 144–160.

**Third Reading**

Right hand alone. Practice using the following combination of legato and staccato. ♪ = 144–160.

**M14-1**

**Fourth Reading**

Left hand alone. ♪ = 144–160.

**Fifth Reading**

Right hand alone. Practice using the following combination of legato and staccato. ♩ = 176–192.

**Sixth Reading**

Hands together. ♩. = 60–69.

**Seventh Reading**

Hands together. Increase the tempo to ♩. = 72–80.

# DRILL A

46

47

# "Perpetual Motion"

T<small>HIS</small> DRILL can sound very effective if you play an accent on the first note of each slur.

**First Reading**
$\eighthnote = 120{-}144$ ( $\quarternote = 60{-}72$ ).

**Second Reading**
$\halfnote = 72{-}84.$

**Third Reading**
$\quarternote = 88{-}100.$

## D<small>RILL</small> B

# "The Harp"

ALTHOUGH this Drill was written to help you develop your left hand technique, the left hand is an accompaniment to the right hand, which has the melody. Play the left-hand part softly enough for the right hand melody to predominate.

**First Reading**
Left hand alone. Play legato and *mf.* ♪ = 120–138 ( ♩=60–69).

**Second Reading**
Left hand alone. Play staccato and *p.*  ♩= 76–88.

**Third Reading**
Right hand alone. Play as written.  ♩= 76–88.

**Fourth Reading**
Hands together. Play the left hand legato and the right hand as written.  ♩= 76–88.

**Fifth Reading**
Hands together. Increase the tempo to  ♩= 96–104.

# DRILL C

# The Old Castle

*From Pictures at an Exhibition*

Modest Mussorgsky

# WEEK
# 5

| | |
|---|---|
| **Monday** | Drill A, First Reading, 5 Minutes<br>Drill B, First Reading, 5 Minutes<br>Drill B, Second Reading, 5 Minutes<br>Drill C, First Reading, 5 Minutes |
| **Tuesday** | Drill A, First Reading, 5 Minutes<br>Drill A, Second Reading, 5 Minutes<br>Drill B, Third Reading, 5 Minutes<br>Drill C, Second Reading, 5 Minutes |
| **Wednesday** | Drill A, Third Reading, 10 Minutes<br>Drill B, Fourth Reading, 5 Minutes<br>Drill C, Third Reading, 5 Minutes |
| **Thursday** | Drill A, Fourth Reading, 5 Minutes<br>Drill B, Fifth Reading, 10 Minutes<br>Drill C, Fourth Reading, 5 Minutes |
| **Friday** | Drill A, Fifth Reading, 5 Minutes<br>Drill B, Sixth Reading, 5 Minutes<br>Drill C, Fifth Reading, 5 Minutes<br>Drill C, Sixth Reading, 5 Minutes |
| **Sat/Sun** | Drill A, Sixth Reading, 5 Minutes<br>Drill B, Seventh Reading, 10 Minutes<br>Drill C, Seventh Reading, 5 Minutes |

# "From Down Under"

THIS DRILL was suggested by Percy Grainger (1882–1961), Australian pianist and composer, for its effectiveness in warming up the hands. For Grainger, practicing this Drill helped to get his hands in condition. After Grainger became an American citizen in 1919, he went on many concert tours throughout North America and abroad.

**First Reading**
Right hand alone. Play *mf.* ♩ = 88–100

**Second Reading**
Left hand alone. Play *mf.* ♩ = 88–100.

**Third Reading**
Hands together. Play *mf.* ♩ = 88–100.

**Fourth Reading**
Hands together. Move both hands up one octave. Play *p.* ♩ = 96–116.

**Fifth Reading**
Hands together. Move the right hand up one octave. Move the left hand down one octave. Play *p.* ♩ = 100–126.

**Sixth Reading**
Hands together. Play as written. Play *mf.* ♩ = 126–138.

# Drill A

# "Three's Company"

WORK for a light, flowing sound in this Drill.

**First Reading**

Right hand alone. ♩ = 72–80.

**Second Reading**

Right hand alone. Play all notes staccato, instead of legato. ♩ = 72–80.

**Third Reading**

Left hand alone. ♩ = 72–80.

**Fourth Reading**

Hands together. ♩ = 72–80.

**Fifth Reading**

Right hand alone. Elongate the first note in each group of three notes and play the remaining two notes rapidly, as indicated in this example.

**Sixth Reading**

Hands together. Play as written. Increase the tempo to ♩ = 96–108.

**Seventh Reading**

Hands together. Increase the tempo to ♩ = 112–126.

# DRILL B

# "Left in the Lurch"

YOU can use this Drill to increase the facility and flexibility of your left hand.

### First Reading

Left hand alone. Play legato and *p*. ♪ = 120–160 ( ♩ = 60–80).

### Second Reading

Left hand alone. Play the following combination of legato and staccato. ♩ = 80–92.

### Third Reading

Left hand alone. Play the following combination of legato and staccato. ♩ = 92–104.

### Fourth Reading

Left hand alone. Play legato. Use the following rhythmic variation. ♩ = 144–168.

### Fifth Reading

Left hand alone. Play legato. Use the following rhythmic variation. ♩ = 144–168.

### Sixth Reading

Right hand alone. ♩ = 92–104.

### Seventh Reading

Hands together. Play as written. ♩ = 96–112.

# Drill C

**Allegro commodo**

64

# Duetto, No. 2

J.S. Bach

69

# WEEK
# 6

| | |
|---|---|
| **Monday** | Drill A, First Reading, 5 Minutes<br>Drill B, First Reading, 5 Minutes<br>Drill C, First Reading, 5 Minutes<br>Drill C, Second Reading, 5 Minutes |
| **Tuesday** | Drill A, Second Reading, 5 Minutes<br>Drill B, First Reading, 5 Minutes<br>Drill C, Third Reading, 10 Minutes |
| **Wednesday** | Drill A, Third Reading, 10 Minutes<br>Drill B, Second Reading, 5 Minutes<br>Drill C, Fourth Reading, 5 Minutes |
| **Thursday** | Drill A, Fourth Reading, 5 Minutes<br>Drill B, Third Reading, 5 Minutes<br>Drill C, Fourth Reading, 5 Minutes<br>Drill C, Fifth Reading, 5 Minutes |
| **Friday** | Drill A, Fifth Reading, 5 Minutes<br>Drill B, Fourth Reading, 5 Minutes<br>Drill C, Sixth Reading, 10 Minutes |
| **Sat/Sun** | Drill A, Sixth Reading, 5 Minutes<br>Drill B, Third Reading, 5 Minutes<br>Drill C, Seventh Reading, 5 Minutes<br>Drill C, Eighth Reading, 5 Minutes |

# "Sewing Machine"

THE ORIGINAL title of this Drill was "Spinning Song." Appropriately, the music has a continuous sixteenth-note motion in each measure. More often, the sixteenth notes are in the form of a trill, with a melody either above or below the trill notes. Play the trill as softly as possible and bring out the melody.

**First Reading**
Right hand alone. ♪ = 116–126

**Second Reading**
Left hand alone. ♪ = 116–126.

**Third Reading**
Hands together. ♪ = 116–126.

**Fourth Reading**
Increase the tempo to ♪ = 132–160.

**Fifth Reading**
Increase the tempo to ♩. = 63–72.

**Sixth Reading**
Increase the tempo to ♩. = 76–88.

# Drill A

73

# "Wrist Relaxer"

IN ORDER to achieve flexibility and control in this Drill, you must let your hands move freely. The palm of the hand will *not* always be parallel to the keyboard. Instead, you will need to turn the hand in order to reach the notes with comfort and ease. Speed is *not* the goal here. You should work for ease.

### First Reading
Right hand alone. Be careful not to squeeze against the keys on the whole notes. Play legato and *p*. ♪ = 80–96.

### Second Reading
Left hand alone. Be careful not to squeeze against the keys on the whole notes. Play legato and *p*. ♪ = 80–96.

### Third Reading
Right hand alone. Increase the tempo to ♪ = 112–120.

### Fourth Reading
Left hand alone. Increase the tempo to ♪ = 112–120.

## Drill B

# "Master of Disguise"

THERE are three sets of fingering for this Drill. The fingerings for each group of two notes, from bottom to top, read as follows: 3 and 2, 4 and 3, and finally, 5 and 4. Most of the two-note slurs in the Drill may be played with one of these pairs of fingers. Your goal is to make the Drill sound exactly the same with each of the three fingerings.

## First Reading

Right hand alone. Use the fingering on the bottom—that is, the third and second finger, unless otherwise noted. ♪ = 112–138.

## Second Reading

Left hand alone. Use the second and third fingers, unless otherwise noted. ♪ = 112–138.

## Third Reading

Hands together. Use the second and third fingers. ♪ = 126–152.

## Fourth Reading

Hands together. Use the third and fourth fingers. ♪ = 126–152.

## Fifth Reading

Hands together. Use the fourth and fifth fingers. ♪ = 126–152.

## Sixth Reading

Select the fingering that is the most difficult for you. Increase the tempo to ♪ = 160–184 ( ♩ = 80–92).

## Seventh Reading

Select the next most difficult fingering and use it throughout. Increase the tempo to ♩ = 80–92.

## Eighth Reading

Use the remaining fingering. ♩ = 80–92.

# Drill C

# Opus 41, No. 44

Zdeněk Fibich

Andante ( ♩ = 80)

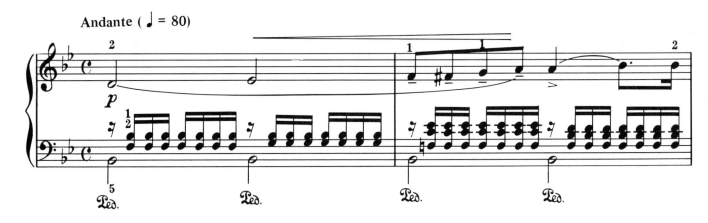

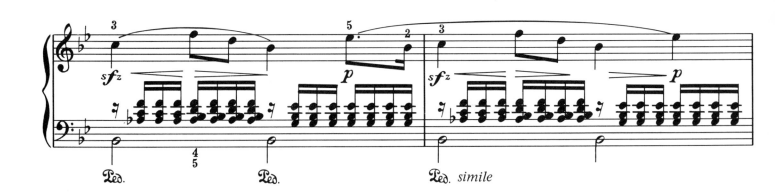

# WEEK
# 7

| | |
|---|---|
| **Monday** | Drill A, First Reading, 5 Minutes<br>Drill B, First Reading, 5 Minutes<br>Drill C, First Reading, 5 Minutes<br>Drill C, Second Reading, 5 Minutes |
| **Tuesday** | Drill A, First Reading, 5 Minutes<br>Drill A, Second Reading, 5 Minutes<br>Drill B, First Reading, 5 Minutes<br>Drill C, Second Reading, 5 Minutes |
| **Wednesday** | Drill A, Third Reading, 5 Minutes<br>Drill B, Second Reading, 5 Minutes<br>Drill C, Third Reading, 5 Minutes<br>Drill C, Fourth Reading, 5 Minutes |
| **Thursday** | Drill A, Fourth Reading, 5 Minutes<br>Drill A, Fifth Reading, 5 Minutes<br>Drill B, Third Reading, 5 Minutes<br>Drill C, Fifth Reading, 5 Minutes |
| **Friday** | Drill A, Sixth Reading, 5 Minutes<br>Drill B, Fourth Reading, 5 Minutes<br>Drill C, Sixth Reading, 10 Minutes |
| **Sat/Sun** | Drill A, Seventh Reading, 10 Minutes<br>Drill B, Fourth Reading, 5 Minutes<br>Drill C, Seventh Reading, 5 Minutes |

THERE are trill-like figures in this Drill that should undulate at a dynamic level softer than that of the melody. Limit the movement of your hands to a minimum when you play these figures.

**First Reading**
Right hand alone. ♪ = 132–152

**Second Reading**
Left hand alone. ♪ = 132–152.

**Third Reading**
Right hand alone. Increase the tempo to ♪ = 168–184.

**Fourth Reading**
Left hand alone. Increase the tempo to ♪ = 168–184.

**Fifth Reading**
Hands together. ♪ = 168–184.

**Sixth Reading**
Hands together. ♩. = 72–80.

**Seventh Reading**
Hands together. Increase the tempo to ♩. = 88–96.

# Drill A

# "Optical Illusion"

AS YOU practice this Drill, do not be tricked by the shifts from treble clef to bass clef, or vice versa. Although the notes may appear to be quite far apart on the page, in reality, they are quite close together (see measure 2 as an example).

**First Reading**
$\eighth = 100\text{--}112$.

**Second Reading**
$\eighth = 112\text{--}126$.

**Third Reading**
$\eighth = 132\text{--}160$.

**Fourth Reading**
$\dotted{\quarter} = 72\text{--}80$.

# Drill B

# "Two for One"

THIS DRILL combines a melody and accompaniment in the right hand. The melody is created by the quarter notes on each beat.

The accompaniment is provided by the sixteenth notes below the quarter notes.

In measures 9–12, the sixteenth notes are featured above the quarter-note melody.

The melody should be played somewhat more loudly than the sixteenth notes of the accompaniment. You can accomplish this by playing the sixteenth notes as quietly as possible and putting a slight accent on the first notes of each beat in the right hand. In order to get an idea of the ideal sound for the right hand, play this excerpt using both hands.

By playing the melody with the right hand and the accompaniment with the left hand, you can make a clear difference in dynamic level between the two parts. The difficulty of this Drill lies in making this difference heard when the right hand plays both parts.

**First Reading**

Right hand alone. Accent the first note of each beat. Play *mf.* ♪ = 86–108.

**Second Reading**

Left hand alone. While the left-hand part may not be particularly difficult, you must know it very well in order to play both hands together. Play *mf.* ♪ = 86–108.

**Third Reading**

Right hand alone. Play *mf.* Increase the tempo to ♪ = 120–144.

**Fourth Reading**

Right hand alone. Play *mf.* Increase the tempo to ♩ = 72–80.

**Fifth Reading**

Hands together. Play *mf.* In order to give yourself a chance to find the notes, slow the tempo to ♪ = 86–108.

**Sixth Reading**

Hands together. Play *mf.* ♪ = 120–144 ( ♩ = 60–72).

**Seventh Reading**

Hands together. Play *mf.* ♩ = 80–88.

# DRILL C

# Scherzo

FELIX MENDELSSOHN

94

# WEEK

# 8

| | |
|---|---|
| **Monday** | Drill A, First Reading, 5 Minutes<br>Drill A, Second Reading, 5 Minutes<br>Drill B, First Reading, 5 Minutes<br>Drill C, First Reading, 5 Minutes |
| **Tuesday** | Drill A, Second Reading, 5 Minutes<br>Drill B, First Reading, 5 Minutes<br>Drill B, Second Reading, 5 Minutes<br>Drill C, First Reading, 5 Minutes |
| **Wednesday** | Drill A, Third Reading, 5 Minutes<br>Drill B, Third Reading, 10 Minutes<br>Drill C, Second Reading, 5 Minutes |
| **Thursday** | Drill A, Fourth Reading, 5 Minutes<br>Drill B, Fourth Reading, 10 Minutes<br>Drill C, Second Reading, 5 Minutes |
| **Friday** | Drill A, Fifth Reading, 5 Minutes<br>Drill A, Sixth Reading, 5 Minutes<br>Drill B, Fifth Reading, 5 Minutes<br>Drill C, Third Reading, 5 Minutes |
| **Sat/Sun** | Drill A, Seventh Reading, 5 Minutes<br>Drill B, Sixth Reading, 10 Minutes<br>Drill C, Third Reading, 5 Minutes |

# "Change Partners and Dance"

REPEATED notes are difficult to play, but they can be made easier if you change fingers on each successive note. As you play this Drill, be sure that you follow the fingerings. Repeated notes must be light and sound separated from each other, even when they are played *f.* In order to achieve this effect, you must keep your fingers and arm so light that they feel as though they are floating on the key. This sensation of floating is the secret to playing staccato. Remember that you can not make the key rise to its surface, but that your fingers must be so light that the action of the key pushes your fingers to the surface of the key, making the note sound staccato.

**First Reading**
Right hand alone. Accent the first note of each beat very slightly. ♪ = 80–96.

**Second Reading**
Right hand alone. Increase the tempo to ♪ = 104–120.

**Third Reading**
Right hand alone. Increase the tempo to ♩ = 60–76.

**Fourth Reading**
Left hand alone. ♩ = 60–76.

**Fifth Reading**
Hands together. Follow the dynamic markings. ♪ = 104–120.

**Sixth Reading**
Hands together. Increase the tempo to ♩ = 60–76.

**Seventh Reading**
Hands together. ♩ = 84–100.

# DRILL A

# "Weaving"

ALTHOUGH each measure of this Drill uses the same musical pattern (alternating major and minor chords), the shape and "feel" of these patterns on the keyboard is quite different in each measure. Concentrate on the difference in "feel" of each measure, moving your hands, arms, and wrists into a comfortable playing position, as necessary.

### First Reading
Right hand alone. The fingering given in the first measure will be used in every measure of this Drill. Play legato and **mp.** ♩ = 66–80 ( ♪ = 132–160).

### Second Reading
Left hand alone. The fingering given in the first measure will be used in every measure of this Drill. Play legato and **mp.** ♩ = 66–80 ( ♪ = 132–160).

### Third Reading
Hands together. Play legato and **mp.** ♩ = 66–80.

### Fourth Reading
Hands together. Play legato and **p.** ♩ = 84–100.

### Fifth Reading
Hands together. Move the right hand up one octave. Move the left hand down one octave. Play legato and **p.** ♩ = 96–120.

### Sixth Reading
Hands together. Play as written. Play leggiero and **mf.** ♩ = 120–132.

# Drill B

101

WEEK 8
## DRILL C

# "Perils of Pauline"

THIS IS a dramatic study for the left hand. Remember that *con fuoco* means "with fire." Although the only dynamic marking is ***ff***, not every note will be equally loud. Nevertheless, ***ff*** does give you a clue to the operatic character of this Drill.

**First Reading**

Be certain that you make a clear difference between staccato and legato. ♪= 132–168.

**Second Reading**

♩= 84–100.

**Third Reading**

♩= 108–120.

# Drill C

# Waltz

### For Robert Abramson

William R. Bauer

Andante ma non troppo ( ♩.= 72-80)

105

106

# Week
# 9

| | |
|---|---|
| **Monday** | Drill A, First Reading, 5 Minutes<br>Drill B, First Reading, 5 Minutes<br>Drill C, First Reading, 10 Minutes |
| **Tuesday** | Drill A, First Reading, 5 Minutes<br>Drill A, Second Reading, 5 Minutes<br>Drill B, Second Reading, 5 Minutes<br>Drill C, First Reading, 5 Minutes |
| **Wednesday** | Drill A, Third Reading, 5 Minutes<br>Drill B, Second Reading, 5 Minutes<br>Drill C, Second Reading, 10 Minutes |
| **Thursday** | Drill A, Fourth Reading, 10 Minutes<br>Drill B, Second Reading, 5 Minutes<br>Drill C, Third Reading, 5 Minutes |
| **Friday** | Drill A, Fourth Reading, 5 Minutes<br>Drill B, Third Reading, 5 Minutes<br>Drill C, Fourth Reading, 5 Minutes<br>Drill C, Fifth Reading, 5 Minutes |
| **Sat/Sun** | Drill A, Fifth Reading, 10 Minutes<br>Drill C, Fifth Reading, 10 Minutes |

# Drill A

# "Swiftly"

WHILE you work on increasing your facility and agility in the right hand, be sure to notice that the curved lines in the left hand are slurs, not ties.

**First Reading**
Right hand alone. Play leggiero. ♪ = 132–152.

**Second Reading**
Right hand alone. Increase the tempo to ♩ = 72–80.

**Third Reading**
Left hand alone. ♩ = 88–100.

**Fourth Reading**
Hands together. ♪ = 120–160 ( ♩ = 60–80).

**Fifth Reading**
Hands together. Increase the tempo to ♩ = 88–100.

# Drill A

THE TEMPO indication—*Andante espressivo*—provides a clue as to how to play this Drill. The melody should sing above the chords of the accompaniment. The pedal will help you connect the notes which you can not sustain with the fingers alone.

**First Reading**

Play the melody alone, as shown below. ♩ = 80–88.

## DRILL B

**Second Reading**

Play as written. ♩ = 72–80.

**Third Reading**

Play as written. Increase the tempo to ♩ = 80–88.

# Drill C

114

# "Rainbows"

THE GOAL of this Drill is to achieve a continuous flow of notes from one hand to the other. If you play *presto* and use the pedal as suggested, the effect is a cascade of sound.

**First Reading**

Hands together. Play legato. ♩ = 104–132.

**Second Reading**

Hands together. Play legato. ♪ = 144–168 ( ♩ = 72–84).

**Third Reading**

Hands together. Play legato. Increase the tempo to ♩ = 96–112.

**Fourth Reading**

Hands together. Play legato. Increase the tempo to ♩ = 120–144.

**Fifth Reading**

Hands together. Play legato. Add the pedal, as suggested ♩ = 120–160.

# Polka, No. 2

### From "Trois Polkas Poétiques," Opus 8

FRIEDRICH SMETANA

118

# WEEK 10

| | |
|---|---|
| **Monday** | Drill A, First Reading, 10 Minutes<br>Drill B, First Reading, 5 Minutes<br>Drill C, First Reading, 5 Minutes |
| **Tuesday** | Drill A, Second Reading, 5 Minutes<br>Drill B, First Reading, 5 Minutes<br>Drill C, Second Reading, 10 Minutes |
| **Wednesday** | Drill A, Second Reading, 5 Minutes<br>Drill A, Third Reading, 5 Minutes<br>Drill B, First Reading, 5 Minutes<br>Drill C, Second Reading, 5 Minutes |
| **Thursday** | Drill A, Fourth Reading, 5 Minutes<br>Drill A, Fifth Reading, 5 Minutes<br>Drill B, Second Reading, 5 Minutes<br>Drill C, Third Reading, 5 Minutes |
| **Friday** | Drill A, Fifth Reading, 5 Minutes<br>Drill A, Sixth Reading, 5 Minutes<br>Drill A, Seventh Reading, 5 Minutes<br>Drill C, Third Reading, 5 Minutes |
| **Sat/Sun** | Drill A, Seventh Reading, 5 Minutes<br>Drill B, Second Reading, 5 Minutes<br>Drill C, Third Reading, 10 Minutes |

# "Long Distance Running"

THIS DRILL is a real workout for the right hand and features a combination of diatonic and chromatic scales, as well as broken chords. The principal difficulty is that the right hand is never relieved from its continuous motion. Since most of your attention will focus on the right hand, you must be certain that you know the left-hand part well.

**First Reading**

Right hand alone. Play legato. $\eighthnote = 100\text{--}120$ ( $\quarternote = 50\text{--}60$).

**Second Reading**

Right hand alone. Use the following combination of legato and staccato. $\quarternote = 66\text{--}80$.

**Third Reading**

Left hand alone. $\quarternote = 66\text{--}80$.

**Fourth Reading**

Right hand alone. Use the following rhythmic variation. Play legato. $\quarternote = 96\text{--}104$.

**Fifth Reading**

Right hand alone. Play as written. $\quarternote = 96\text{--}104$.

**Sixth Reading**

Left hand alone. $\quarternote = 96\text{--}104$.

**Seventh Reading**

Hands together. $\quarternote = 96\text{--}104$.

# Drill A

# "Combinations"

THE NOTES with two stems found in this Drill (shown in the squares in the example below), are to be held as quarter notes. They should also be stressed, as indicated, by *tenuti* added to the score. If you remember to play these notes *cantabile*—that is, in a singing style—you will discover the proper sound for this Drill.

**First Reading**
 ♪ = 120–144 ( ♩ = 60–72).

**Second Reading**
 ♩ = 72–76.

# Drill B

# "Duet"

WHEN YOU have learned this Drill, it should sound as if it were a melody, perhaps played on a flute or violin and accompanied by a harp.

**First Reading**

Play the melody alone with the right hand, as shown below. Play legato and **mp.**  ♩ = 66–72.

**Second Reading**

Play the chords alone, as shown below. Each chord should not be rolled too quickly. Similarly, the grace notes are not to be played too fast. Change the pedal on the lowest note of each chord.  ♩ = 66–72.

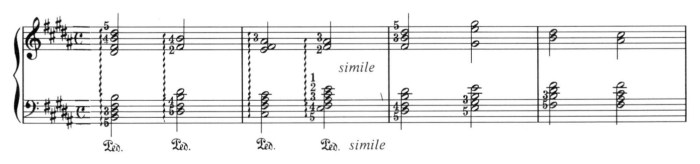

**Third Reading**

Play as written. Be careful not to roll the chords too quickly. They must sound expressive. ♩ = 66–72.

# Drill C

# Trois Écossaises

## Opus 72, Nos. 3–5

FRÉDÉRIC CHOPIN

130

# "Tails Up"

THIS DRILL is an excellent way to help you gain control over your third and fourth fingers. The alternation of notes which are closely spaced on the keyboard with notes which are more widely spaced make the Drill an excellent warm-up exercise.

### First Reading

Left hand alone. Decide for yourself if you would like to observe the repeat signs. In certain measures, you may feel the need for a little extra workout. Play legato and **mp**. ♪ = 100–132.

### Second Reading

Right hand alone. Play legato and **mp**. ♪ = 100–132.

### Third Reading

Hands together. Play legato and **mp**. ♪ = 100–132.

### Fourth Reading

Right hand alone. Play the complete Drill using each of the rhythmic variations shown below. In each case, hold the note with the fermata (⌒) as long as you need in order to collect your thoughts, so that you can play the other notes quickly. Play legato and **mp**.

### Fifth Reading

Left hand alone. Follow the directions for the Fourth Reading.

### Sixth Reading

Hands together. Play staccato and **f**. ♪ = 144–168 ( ♩ = 72–84).

### Seventh Reading

Hands together. Play staccato and **p**. ♩ = 80–100.

# Drill A

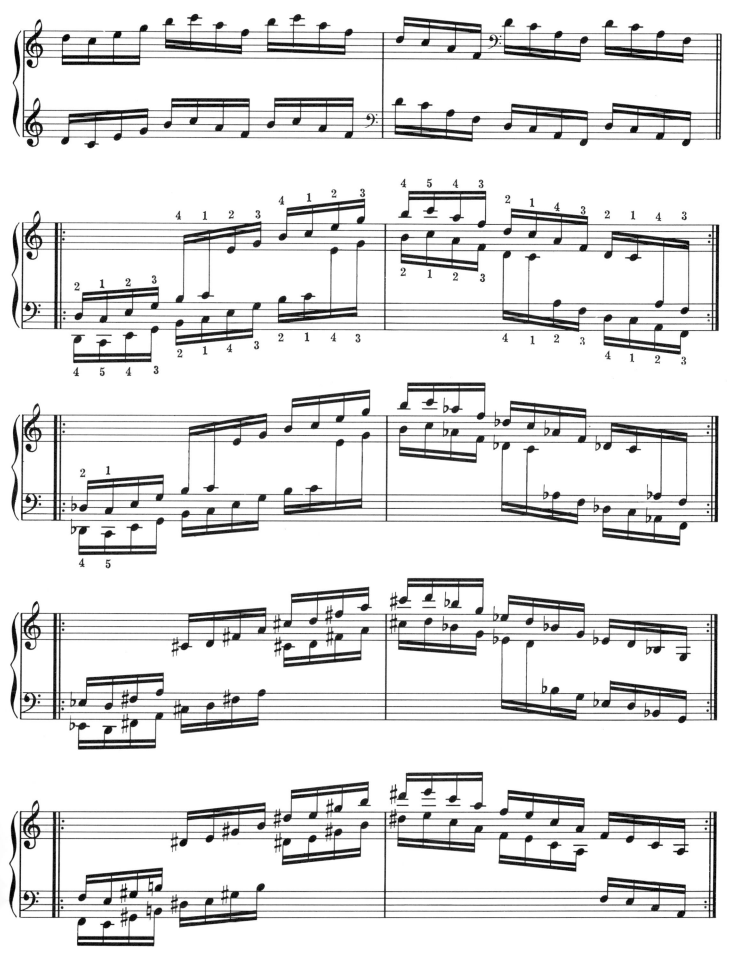

136

# WEEK
# 11

| | |
|---|---|
| **Monday** | Drill A, First Reading, 5 Minutes<br>Drill A, Second Reading, 5 Minutes<br>Drill B, First Reading, 5 Minutes<br>Drill C, First Reading, 5 Minutes |
| **Tuesday** | Drill A, First Reading, 5 Minutes<br>Drill A, Second Reading, 5 Minutes<br>Drill B, Second Reading, 5 Minutes<br>Drill C, First Reading, 5 Minutes |
| **Wednesday** | Drill A, Third Reading, 10 Minutes<br>Drill B, Third Reading, 5 Minutes<br>Drill C, Second Reading, 5 Minutes |
| **Thursday** | Drill A, Fourth Reading, 5 Minutes<br>Drill A, Fifth Reading, 5 Minutes<br>Drill B, Fourth Reading, 5 Minutes<br>Drill C, Third Reading, 5 Minutes |
| **Friday** | Drill A, Sixth Reading, 10 Minutes<br>Drill B, Fifth Reading, 5 Minutes<br>Drill C, Fourth Reading, 5 Minutes |
| **Sat/Sun** | Drill A, Sixth Reading, 5 Minutes<br>Drill A, Seventh Reading, 5 Minutes<br>Drill B, Sixth Reading, 5 Minutes<br>Drill C, Fourth Reading, 5 Minutes |

# "Double Up"

LEGATO thirds are not too difficult to play if the notes all lie within one finger group, as shown.

However, when there is a change in the finger group, it is not possible to connect both notes from one third to another. In this example, you can connect the top notes only.

When the second pair of notes are below the first pair, you can connect only the bottom notes.

**First Reading**
Right hand alone. Play legato, remembering the discussion presented above. Play *mf.* ♪ = 104–116.

**Second Reading**
Right hand alone. Increase the tempo to ♪ = 126–160.

**Third Reading**
Right hand alone. Increase the tempo to ♪ = 168–180.

**Fourth Reading**
Right hand alone. ♩. = 60–72.

**Fifth Reading**
Left hand alone. ♩. = 60–72.

**Sixth Reading**
Hands together. ♩. = 60–80.

# Drill B

# "Boogie Bass"

**First Reading**
Play *mf.* ♪ = 152–168.

**Second Reading**
Play staccato and *p.* ♪ = 176–192.

**Third Reading**
Play *f.* ♩. = 60–68.

**Fourth Reading**
Play *mp.* Increase the tempo to ♩. = 72–84.

## DRILL C

# Scherzino

## Opus 39, No. 11

EDWARD MACDOWELL

# Week 12

| | |
|---|---|
| **Monday** | Drill A, First Reading, 5 Minutes<br>Drill A, Second Reading, 5 Minutes<br>Drill B, First Reading, 5 Minutes<br>Drill C, First Reading, 5 Minutes |
| **Tuesday** | Drill A, First Reading, 5 Minutes<br>Drill B, Second Reading, 5 Minutes<br>Drill B, Third Reading, 5 Minutes<br>Drill C, Second Reading, 5 Minutes |
| **Wednesday** | Drill A, Second Reading, 5 Minutes<br>Drill B, Third Reading, 5 Minutes<br>Drill C, Third Reading, 5 Minutes<br>Drill C, Fourth Reading, 5 Minutes |
| **Thursday** | Drill A, Third Reading, 5 Minutes<br>Drill B, Fourth Reading, 5 Minutes<br>Drill C, Fourth Reading, 10 Minutes |
| **Friday** | Drill A, Fourth Reading, 5 Minutes<br>Drill B, Fifth Reading, 5 Minutes<br>Drill B, Sixth Reading, 5 Minutes<br>Drill C, Fifth Reading, 5 Minutes |
| **Sat/Sun** | Drill A, Fifth Reading, 10 Minutes<br>Drill A, Fifth Reading, 5 Minutes<br>Drill C, Fifth Reading, 5 Minutes |

# "Light as a Feather"

THIS DRILL will help you develop greater finger independence and control. The fingering is the same in measures 1–10. A new pattern occurs in measures 11–21. The dotted quarter notes should be held down as lightly as possible. After you play these notes, do not squeeze against the keys. In this way, you will be able to play the sixteenth notes with ease. If your hand does not comfortably span the sixteenth notes while holding down the dotted quarter notes, you may release the dotted quarter notes sooner than indicated. Remember, the goal in this Drill is *control,* not speed.

**First Reading**

Left hand alone. Play legato and *mf.* ♪ = 92–112.

**Second Reading**

Right hand alone. Play legato and *mf.* ♪ = 92–112.

**Third Reading**

Left hand alone. Play staccato. ♪ = 116–132.

**Fourth Reading**

Right hand alone. Play staccato. ♪ = 116–132.

**Fifth Reading**

Hands together. Play legato. ♪ = 116–132.

# Drill A

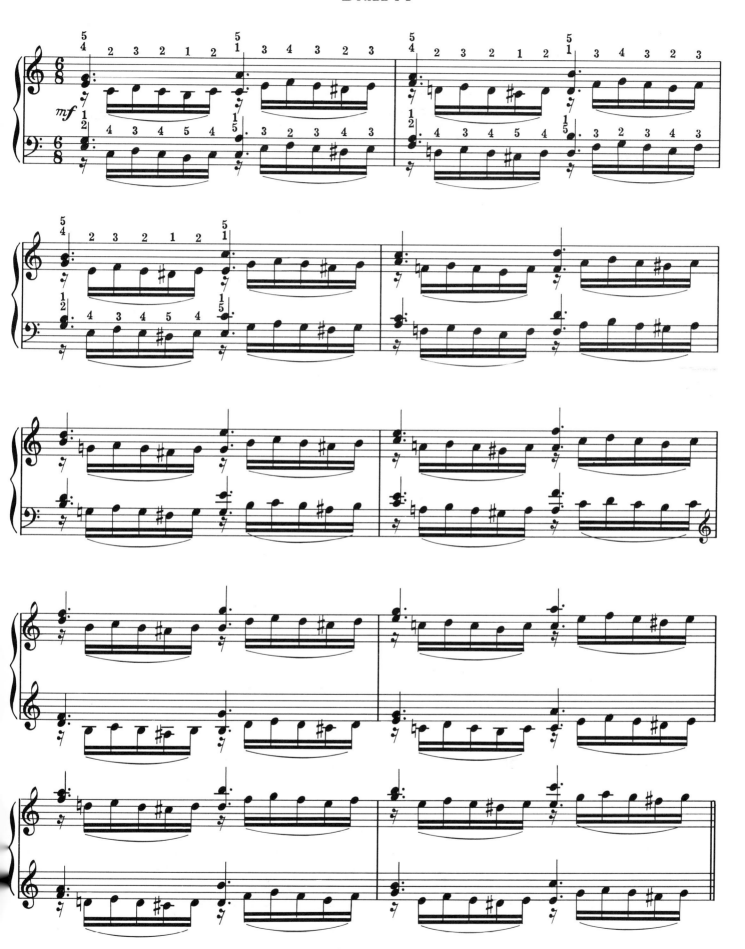

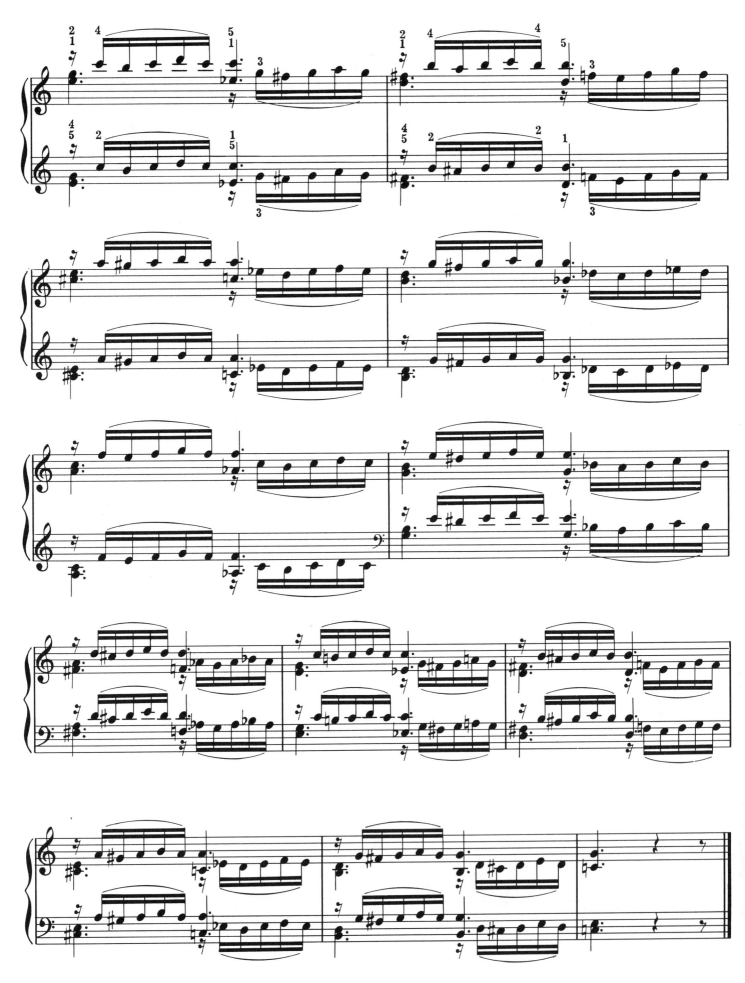

# "Fourth Place"

SINCE the fourths in this Drill occur in pairs, they are easy to connect. In measures 6–8, cross the left hand over the right hand.

**First Reading**

Right hand alone. Play *mf.* ♪ = 116–132.

**Second Reading**

Left hand alone. Play *mf.* ♪ = 116–132.

**Third Reading**

Hands together. Play *mf.* ♪ = 116–132.

**Fourth Reading**

Hands together. Play *p.* ♪ = 144–168 ( ♩ = 72–84).

**Fifth Reading**

Hands together. Move the right hand up one octave. Move the left hand down one octave. ♩ = 72–84.

**Sixth Reading**

Play as written. Play *f.* Increase the tempo to ♩ = 88–100.

# Drill B

ALTHOUGH the entire right-hand part of this Drill is notated using thirty-second notes, you should not be intimidated by these many black notes. The thirty-second notes in this piece need not be played very quickly. Although the time signature given is $\frac{2}{4}$, you should think of the music in $\frac{4}{8}$ (four eighth notes per measure with each note equivalent to one beat). Thus, you can feel the four thirty-second notes per beat in the same way that you feel the four sixteenth notes per beat in $\frac{4}{4}$ time.

In this Drill, you will work on developing the outer extremities of your right hand—the fourth and fifth fingers and the thumb and second fingers.

**First Reading**

Right hand alone. Play legato and *p*. ♪ = 72–80.

**Second Reading**

Left hand alone. Concentrate on making the eighth notes as expressive as possible. Play legato. ♪ = 72–80.

**Third Reading**

Right hand alone. Increase the tempo to ♪ = 92–104.

**Fourth Reading**

Hands together. ♪ = 66–80.

**Fifth Reading**

Hands together. Increase the tempo to ♪ = 92–104.

# Drill C

# Adagio in B Minor

W.A. MOZART

155

# WEEK 13

| | |
|---|---|
| **Monday** | Drill A, First Reading, 5 Minutes<br>Drill A, Second Reading, 5 Minutes<br>Drill B, First Reading, 5 Minutes<br>Drill C, First Reading, 5 Minutes |
| **Tuesday** | Drill A, First Reading, 5 Minutes<br>Drill A, Second Reading, 5 Minutes<br>Drill B, First Reading, 5 Minutes<br>Drill C, Second Reading, 5 Minutes |
| **Wednesday** | Drill A, Third Reading, 10 Minutes<br>Drill B, Second Reading, 5 Minutes<br>Drill C, Third Reading, 5 Minutes |
| **Thursday** | Drill A, Fourth Reading, 5 Minutes<br>Drill B, Third Reading, 5 Minutes<br>Drill C, Third Reading, 5 Minutes<br>Drill C, Fourth Reading, 5 Minutes |
| **Friday** | Drill A, Fifth Reading, 5 Minutes<br>Drill B, Fourth Reading, 5 Minutes<br>Drill C, Fifth Reading, 5 Minutes<br>Drill C, Sixth Reading, 5 Minutes |
| **Sat/Sun** | Drill A, Fifth Reading, 10 Minutes<br>Drill B, Fourth Reading, 5 Minutes<br>Drill C, Seventh Reading, 5 Minutes |

# "Sharp and Flat"

THIS DRILL focuses on chromatic scales—played by each hand individually, using hands together, and in contrary motion. Aim to play this Drill with as much agility as possible.

**First Reading**

Left hand alone. ♪ = 120–144 ( ♩ = 60–72).

**Second Reading**

Right hand alone. ♪ = 120–144 ( ♩ = 60–72).

**Third Reading**

Hands together. ♪ = 120–144 ( ♩ = 60–72).

**Fourth Reading**

Hands together. Increase the tempo to ♩ = 80–96.

**Fifth Reading**

Hands together. Increase the tempo to ♩ = 100–120.

# Drill A

162

OCTAVES occurring on black keys are most often played with the thumb and fourth finger, rather than with the thumb and fifth finger. If this fingering is not comfortable for you, you may play all octaves with the thumb and fifth finger.

**First Reading**
  ♪ = 112–126.

**Second Reading**
  ♪ = 132–160.

**Third Reading**
  ♩. = 72–80.

**Fourth Reading**
  ♩. = 96–104.

# Drill B

**Allegro**

THERE is a similarity between this Drill by Czerny and the famous "Butterfly" etude by Chopin (Opus 25, No. 9)—each of these two pieces has a rather thick texture, and yet they must sound light and "flutter." Do not play this Drill too loudly.

**First Reading**
Right hand alone. ♪ = 88–108.

**Second Reading**
Right hand alone. Increase the tempo to ♩ = 144–160 ( ♩ = 72–80).

**Third Reading**
Right hand alone. Use the following rhythmic variation. ♩ = 108–120.

**Fourth Reading**
Left hand alone. ♩ = 72–80.

**Fifth Reading**
Right hand alone. Play the following variation. Hold the whole notes down as lightly as possible, so that you have freedom to play the quarter notes. ♩ = 72–80.

**Sixth Reading**
Hands together. Play as written. ♩ = 72–80.

**Seventh Reading**
Hands together. Increase the tempo to ♩ = 96–104.

# DRILL C

# Prelude No. 8

DMITRI SHOSTAKOVICH

Allegretto ( ♩ = 104-112)

# WEEK 14

| | |
|---|---|
| **Monday** | Drill A, First Reading, 10 Minutes<br>Drill B, First Reading, 10 Minutes |
| **Tuesday** | Drill C, First Reading, 5 Minutes<br>Drill C, Second Reading, 5 Minutes<br>Drill A, First Reading, 5 Minutes<br>Drill B, First Reading, 5 Minutes |
| **Wednesday** | Drill A, Second Reading, 5 Minutes<br>Drill B, Second Reading, 5 Minutes<br>Drill C, First Reading, 5 Minutes<br>Drill C, Second Reading, 5 Minutes |
| **Thursday** | Drill A, Third Reading, 5 Minutes<br>Drill B, Third Reading, 5 Minutes<br>Drill C, Third Reading, 10 Minutes |
| **Friday** | Drill A, Fourth Reading, 5 Minutes<br>Drill B, Fourth Reading, 5 Minutes<br>Drill C, Second Reading, 5 Minutes<br>Drill C, Third Reading, 5 Minutes |
| **Sat/Sun** | Drill A, Fourth Reading, 10 Minutes<br>Drill B, Fourth Reading, 5 Minutes<br>Drill C, Third Reading, 10 Minutes |

# "Criss-Cross"

THIS DRILL concentrates on the skill of crossing the hands one over the other to play a chord. To help yourself find the correct notes, concentrate on the thumb rather than the fifth finger as you cross each over the other.

**First Reading**
    Both hands. Play as written. ♪ = 76–92.

**Second Reading**
    Both hands. Play as written. ♪ = 92–108.

**Third Reading**
    Both hands. Play as written. ♪ = 116–138.

**Fourth Reading**
    Both hands. Play as written. ♪ = 144–168.

## Drill A

# "Close Procession"

THIS DRILL concentrates on the problem of playing interlocking octaves—that is, octaves that alternate from one hand to the other. Most measures in the Drill are based on chromatic scales. However, measure 5 is a C major scale and measure 11 outlines a C major chord. Focus your attention on the thumbs of each hand. As you alternate from one hand to the other, the thumbs are always the fingers closest to each other. It would be much more difficult if you directed your attention to the fifth fingers, because they are much further away from each other.

**First Reading**

Hands together. Play staccato and *f,* as marked. ♪ = 80–96.

**Second Reading**

Hands together. Play staccato and *f.* ♪ = 100–126.

**Third Reading**

Hands together. Play staccato and *f.* ♪ = 132–160.

**Fourth Reading**

Hands together. Play staccato and *f.* Increase the tempo to ♪ = 168–192.

# DRILL B

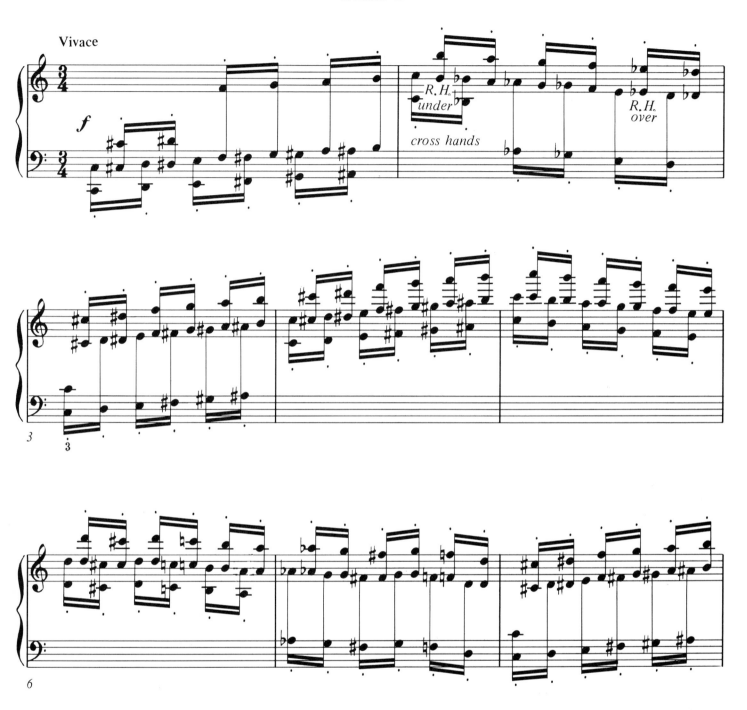

# "Slides"

A GLISSANDO is a rapid scale, played by drawing the nail of the second or third finger over the white keys. This technique is accomplished by inverting the hand over the keys, and is appropriate only to ascending glissandi that occur on the white keys, played with the right hand.

In the left hand, an ascending glissando that occurs on the white keys is played with the thumb nail.

**Right Hand:**                    **Left Hand:**

Right-hand descending glissandi that occur on the white keys are played with the nail of the thumb. Descending glissandi in the left hand require the use of the nail of the third finger.

A glissando on the black keys is played with the side of the second finger rather than the nail. You must be careful to execute a glissando on the white keys using only the tip of the nail, allowing no part of the skin to come in contact with the key. Do not bear down too much. Instead, allow the hand to glide over the surface of the keys.

This "Sarabande" contains several glissandi. Composer William Bauer wrote it especially for the *20 Minute Piano Workout*. A *sarabande* is a slow, dignified dance, originally popular during the seventeenth and eighteenth centuries. Sarabandes always have three beats to the measure, with a stress on the second beat. This sarabande is a modern one, but it has the same characteristics as the original dances of this kind.

**First Reading**
Hands together. Play as written, except eliminate all glissandi. ♩ = 69.

**Second Reading**
Play only the glissandi taken from "Sarabande," as shown in the following example.

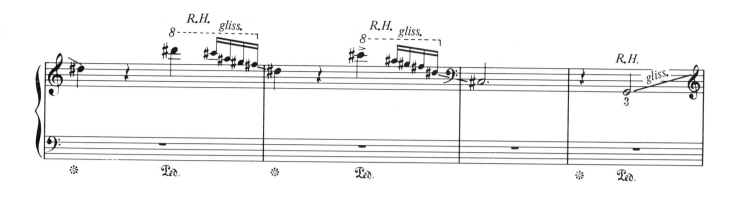

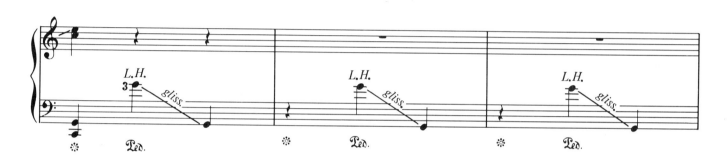

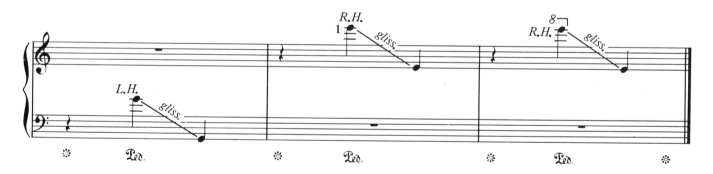

**Third Reading**

Play as written. ♩ = 69

DRILL C

# Sarabande

William Bauer

With sad dignity ( ♩ = 69)

178

179

# Prelude in C

## Opus 12, No. 7

SERGEI PROKOFIEFF

# WEEK
# 15

| | |
|---|---|
| **Monday** | Drill A, First Reading, 10 Minutes<br>Drill B, First Reading, 5 Minutes<br>Drill C, First Reading, 5 Minutes |
| **Tuesday** | Drill A, First Reading, 5 Minutes<br>Drill A, Second Reading, 5 Minutes<br>Drill C, First Reading, 5 Minutes<br>Drill C, Second Reading, 5 Minutes |
| **Wednesday** | Drill A, Third Reading, 5 Minutes<br>Drill B, Second Reading, 5 Minutes<br>Drill C, Second Reading, 5 Minutes<br>Drill C, Third Reading, 5 Minutes |
| **Thursday** | Drill A, Fourth Reading, 5 Minutes<br>Drill B, Third Reading, 5 Minutes<br>Drill C, Third Reading, 5 Minutes<br>Drill C, Fourth Reading, 5 Minutes |
| **Friday** | Drill A, Fifth Reading, 10 Minutes<br>Drill B, Fourth Reading, 5 Minutes<br>Drill C, Fifth Reading, 5 Minutes |
| **Sat/Sun** | Drill A, Sixth Reading, 5 Minutes<br>Drill B, Fourth Reading, 5 Minutes<br>Drill C, Fifth Reading, 10 Minutes |

# "Eight Is Enough"

REMEMBER that octaves that occur on the black keys are often played with the fourth finger, or even the third finger. If either of these fingerings is preferable to you, do not hesitate to change the fingerings shown.

**First Reading**

Hands together. Play each pair of octaves simultaneously throughout the Drill, as shown in the following example. ♩=66–76.

**Second Reading**

Hands together. Play each pair of octaves as a two-note slur throughout the Drill, as shown in the following example. ♩=66–76.

**Third Reading**

Hands together. Play the Drill using staccato, as written. ♩=66–72.

**Fourth Reading**

Hands together. Play each pair of octaves in the reverse order throughout the Drill—playing the top note first, followed by the lower note, as shown in the following example. ♩=66–72.

**Fifth Reading**

Hands together. Play as written. Increase the tempo to ♩=84–100.

**Sixth Reading**

Hands together. Increase the tempo to ♩=104–112.

# DRILL A

189

190

# "A Pause for the Paws"

**First Reading**
♪ = 120–144.

**Second Reading**
♪ = 152–168.

**Third Reading**
♪ = 176–192.

**Fourth Reading**
♩. = 60–72.

## DRILL B

# "Fanfare"

THIS IS a more challenging version of the problem found in Drill A, Week 14. As you play this Drill, remember to keep your eye on your thumb, not on your fifth finger. Memorize the fingering for each chord.

**First Reading**
Right hand alone. Play staccato and *f,* as marked. ♪= 80–104.

**Second Reading**
Left hand alone. Play staccato and *f,* as marked. ♪= 80–104.

**Third Reading**
Hands together. Play staccato and *f.* ♪= 80–104.

**Fourth Reading**
Hands together. Play staccato and *f.* ♪= 108–126.

**Fifth Reading**
Hands together. Play staccato and *f.* ♪= 132–160.

# Drill C

# June

### From The Seasons
### Opus 37, No. 6

PETER ILICH TCHAIKOVSKY

Andante cantabile ( ♩ = 80-84)

196

198

# WEEK
# 16

| | |
|---|---|
| **Monday** | Drill A, First Reading, 5 Minutes<br>Drill B, First Reading, 5 Minutes<br>Drill B, Second Reading, 5 Minutes<br>Drill C, First Reading, 5 Minutes |
| **Tuesday** | Drill A, First Reading, 5 Minutes<br>Drill A, Second Reading, 5 Minutes<br>Drill B, Third Reading, 10 Minutes |
| **Wednesday** | Drill A, Third Reading, 5 Minutes<br>Drill B, Third Reading, 5 Minutes<br>Drill C, First Reading, 5 Minutes<br>Drill C, Second Reading, 5 Minutes |
| **Thursday** | Drill A, Fourth Reading, 5 Minutes<br>Drill A, Fifth Reading, 5 Minutes<br>Drill B, Fourth Reading, 5 Minutes<br>Drill C, Third Reading, 5 Minutes |
| **Friday** | Drill A, Sixth Reading, 5 Minutes<br>Drill A, Seventh Reading, 5 Minutes<br>Drill B, Fifth Reading, 5 Minutes<br>Drill C, Third Reading, 5 Minutes |
| **Sat/Sun** | Drill A, Seventh Reading, 10 Minutes<br>Drill B, Sixth Reading, 5 Minutes<br>Drill C, Fourth Reading, 5 Minutes |

MOUNT PARNASSUS was the home of the ancient Greek gods. As such, it represented the pinnacle of understanding and perfection. Muzio Clementi knew that every pianist wanted to have a godlike level of perfection in their playing and, for this reason, named his piano studies *Gradus ad Parnassum* (Steps to Parnassus). This Drill can help you develop your fourth and fifth fingers. Clementi was exacting in his design of this Drill. You must use both the fourth and fifth fingers in each measure. Be sure to keep your arm as light as possible—that is, do not bear downward with the arm. Instead, it should seem as though the arm is floating. Keep in mind that, as you depress each key, you do not need to push the key all the way down to the key bed. Depress the key just to the point where you hear the sound, which occurs before the key bed.

**First Reading**
> Right hand alone. Play legato and **p.**  ♪= 84–108.

**Second Reading**
> Right hand alone. Play legato and **p.**  ♩= 66–76.

**Third Reading**
> Right hand alone. Play each measure using the combination of legato and staccato shown below.  ♩= 76–88.

**Fourth Reading**
> Left hand alone.  ♩= 76–88.

**Fifth Reading**
> Hands together. Play the right hand legato  ♪= 144–168 ( ♩= 72–84).

**Sixth Reading**
> Right hand alone. Use the following rhythmic variation throughout. Play legato.

M75-2

**Seventh Reading**
> Hands together. Play the right hand legato, as written. Increase the tempo to  ♩= 100–120.

# Drill A

# "Quick Switch"

AS YOU play this Drill, try to achieve as much agility as possible.

**First Reading**
Right hand alone. ♪= 120–144.

**Second Reading**
Left hand alone. ♪= 120–144.

**Third Reading**
Hands together. ♪= 120–144.

**Fourth Reading**
Hands together. Play all sixteenth notes with the following combination of legato and staccato. ♩= 72–80.

**Fifth Reading**
Hands together. Play all sixteenth notes legato. Increase the tempo to ♩= 92–108.

**Sixth Reading**
Increase the tempo to ♩= 112–120.

# DRILL B

# "At the Hop"

WHEN playing this Drill, keep in mind that *Allegro non troppo* means "fast, but not too fast." The two-note slurs should be played with a slight stress on the first note, with the second note slightly shorter than the first.

**First Reading**
 ♪ = 96–104.

**Second Reading**
 ♪ = 120–132.

**Third Reading**
 ♩ = 66–72.

**Fourth Reading**
 ♩ = 76–80.

# Drill C

# La plus que lente

*Valse*

CLAUDE DEBUSSY

Lento *(Molto rubato con morvidezza)* (♩ = 126-138)

sostenuto       a tempo (Rubato)

cresc.

dim. molto

stringendo

dim.

p

leggero

# WEEK
# 17

| | |
|---|---|
| **Monday** | Drill A, First Reading, 5 Minutes<br>Drill A, Second Reading, 5 Minutes<br>Drill B, First Reading, 5 Minutes<br>Drill C, First Reading, 5 Minutes |
| **Tuesday** | Drill A, Second Reading, 5 Minutes<br>Drill A, Third Reading, 5 Minutes<br>Drill B, First Reading, 5 Minutes<br>Drill C, Second Reading, 5 Minutes |
| **Wednesday** | Drill A, Fourth Reading, 10 Minutes<br>Drill B, Second Reading, 5 Minutes<br>Drill C, Third Reading, 5 Minutes |
| **Thursday** | Drill A, Fifth Reading, 5 Minutes<br>Drill A, Third Reading, 5 Minutes<br>Drill C, Fourth Reading, 10 Minutes |
| **Friday** | Drill A, Sixth Reading, 5 Minutes<br>Drill B, Fourth Reading, 5 Minutes<br>Drill C, Fifth Reading, 5 Minutes<br>Drill C, Sixth Reading, 5 Minutes |
| **Sat/Sun** | Drill A, Sixth Reading, 10 Minutes<br>Drill B, Fourth Reading, 5 Minutes<br>Drill C, Sixth Reading, 5 Minutes |

# "Triplets"

THIS DRILL should sound like a scherzo by Mendelssohn—light and presto.

**First Reading**
Left hand alone. ♪ = 96–116.

**Second Reading**
Right hand alone. ♪ = 96–116.

**Third Reading**
Right hand alone. Increase the tempo to ♪ = 126–152.

**Fourth Reading**
Hands together. ♪ = 96–116.

**Fifth Reading**
Hands together. Increase the tempo to ♪ = 144–168 ( ♩ = 72–84).

**Sixth Reading**
Hands together. ♩ = 88–96.

# Drill A

**Allegro molto agitato**

218

# "Crawling"

THIS DRILL is based on the chromatic scale, but it is also a dramatic piece of music. The key to the mood is found in the indication: *Allegro risoluto,* meaning fast and in a vigorous and decided style.

**First Reading**
♪ = 92–100.

**Second Reading**
♪ = 108–126.

**Third Reading**
♪ = 126–144.

**Fourth Reading**
♪ = 152–160.

# Drill B

# "Wrist Oil"

MEASURES 1–4 and 11–16 are not too difficult to play if you repeat the chords using a wrist motion. Do not attempt to play legato, except as marked.

**First Reading**
Right hand alone.  ♩ = 66–76.

**Second Reading**
Right hand alone.  ♩ = 76–84.

**Third Reading**
Left hand alone.  ♩ = 76–84.

**Fourth Reading**
Hands together.  ♩ = 76–84.

**Fifth Reading**
Hands together. Increase the tempo to  ♩ = 92–96.

**Sixth Reading**
Hands together.  ♩ = 100–112.

# DRILL C

# March of the Trolls

## Opus 54, No. 3

EDVARD GRIEG

Allegro moderato ( ♩ = 116-120)

228

230

# WEEK 18

| | |
|---|---|
| **Monday** | Drill A, First Reading, 5 Minutes<br>Drill B, First Reading, 5 Minutes<br>Drill C, First Reading, 5 Minutes<br>Drill C, Second Reading, 5 Minutes |
| **Tuesday** | Drill A, Second Reading, 5 Minutes<br>Drill B, First Reading, 5 Minutes<br>Drill B, Second Reading, 5 Minutes<br>Drill C, Second Reading, 5 Minutes |
| **Wednesday** | Drill A, Third Reading, 5 Minutes<br>Drill A, Fourth Reading, 5 Minutes<br>Drill C, Third Reading, 5 Minutes<br>Drill C, Fourth Reading, 5 Minutes |
| **Thursday** | Drill A, Fourth Reading, 5 Minutes<br>Drill B, Third Reading, 5 Minutes<br>Drill C, Fifth Reading, 5 Minutes<br>Drill C, Sixth Reading, 5 Minutes |
| **Friday** | Drill A, Fifth Reading, 5 Minutes<br>Drill A, Sixth Reading, 5 Minutes<br>Drill B, Fourth Reading, 5 Minutes<br>Drill C, Seventh Reading, 5 Minutes |
| **Sat/Sun** | Drill A, Seventh Reading, 5 Minutes<br>Drill B, Fifth Reading, 5 Minutes<br>Drill C, Seventh Reading, 5 Minutes<br>Drill C, Eighth Reading, 5 Minutes |

# "In Tandem"

### First Reading
Right hand alone. Play legato. ♪= 120–144.

### Second Reading
Left hand alone. Play legato. ♪= 120–144.

### Third Reading
Hands together. Play legato. ♪= 120–144.

### Fourth Reading
Hands together. Play staccato. ♪= 160–184 ( ♩ = 80–92).

### Fifth Reading
Hands together. Use the following combination of legato and staccato in both hands. ♩= 96–100.

**M84-1**

### Sixth Reading
Hands together. Use the following combination of staccato and legato. ♩= 96–100.

**M84-2**

### Seventh Reading
Hands together. Play legato. Increase the tempo to ♩= 112–126.

# DRILL A

WEEK 18
## DRILL B

# "Alternating Current"

DRILL B is similar to Drill C, Week 2. In that Drill, scales were divided between the two hands, with each hand playing successive notes. Here, the scale notes are harmonized in measures 1–6. The other measures call for alternating hands in other patterns.

**First Reading**

Hands together. Play legato. ♪= 96–108.

**Second Reading**

Hands together. Play staccato. ♪= 96–108.

**Third Reading**

Hands together. Play legato. Increase the tempo to ♪= 120–144 ( ♩= 60–72).

**Fourth Reading**

Hands together. ♩= 80–96.

**Fifth Reading**

Hands together. ♩= 100–112.

# DRILL B

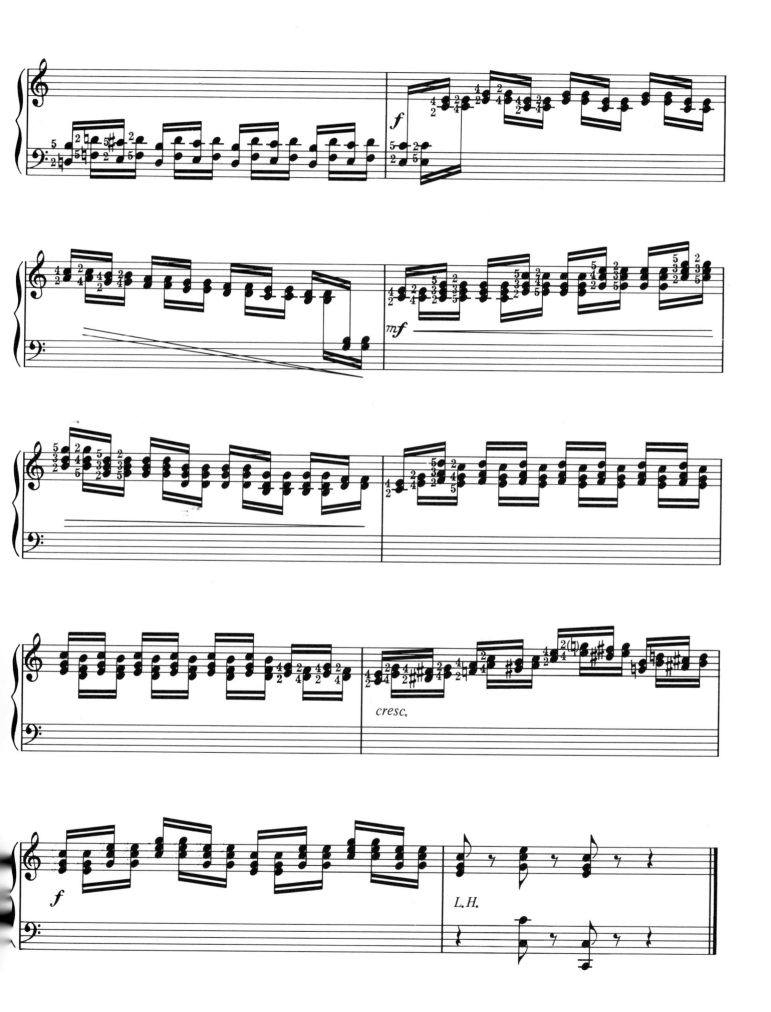

# "Leading Tones"

IN THIS DRILL, you will develop your control of the third, fourth, and fifth fingers.

**First Reading**
Right hand alone. ♩=66–76.

**Second Reading**
Right hand alone. Increase the tempo to ♩=80–88.

**Third Reading**
Right hand alone. Play staccato. ♩=80–88.

**Fourth Reading**
Left hand alone. ♩=80–88.

**Fifth Reading**
Hands together. ♩=80–88.

**Sixth Reading**
Right hand alone. Practice the following combination of legato and staccato. ♩=96–100.

**Seventh Reading**
Right hand alone. Practice the following variation. ♩=80–88.

**Eighth Reading**
Hands together, as written. ♩=112–132.

# DRILL C

Allegro agitato

241

242

243

244

# The Sussex Mummers' Christmas Carol

ARRANGED BY PERCY ALDRIDGE GRAINGER

Slowish, but flowing ( ♪ = between 84 and 100.)

*The Tune, printed in big notes, should through-
out be brought out with a rich piercing tone and
heard well above the accompanying parts. P.A.G.